"AHH!

said stork

"Ahhh!" said stork. "I will eat this egg."
He pecked at it but it would not break. All the
other animals tried, but it still would not break.
Then, one day, they saw that the egg
had a tiny crack . . . .

"AHHH!"
said stork

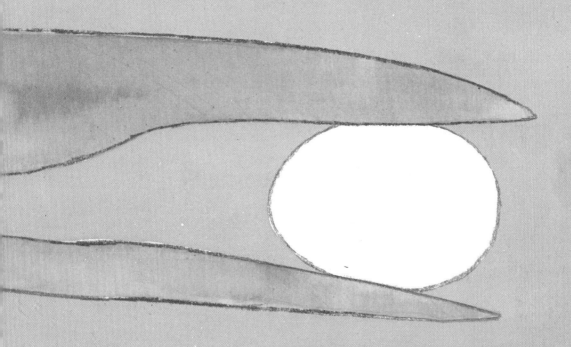

Gerald Rose

MACMILLAN CHILDREN'S BOOKS

"Ahhh!" said stork.
"I will eat this egg."
He pecked at it but it would not break.

Hippopotamus rolled on it.

Lion bit it.

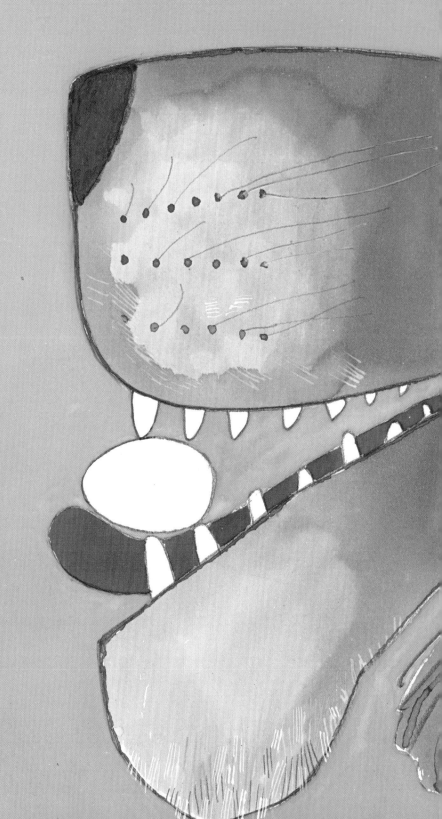

Chimp hit it.

Elephant stamped on it.

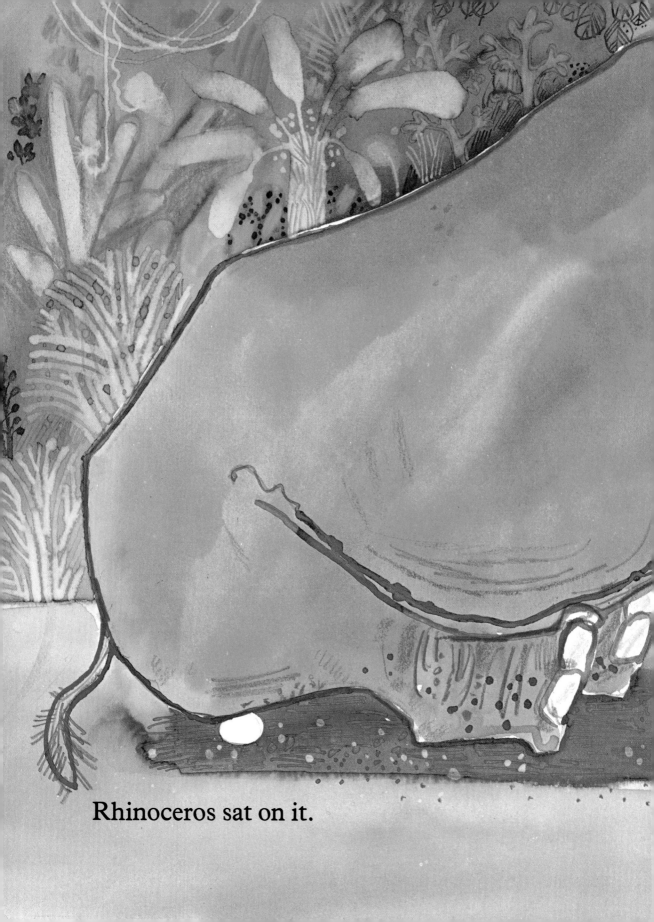

Rhinoceros sat on it.

Snake squeezed it.

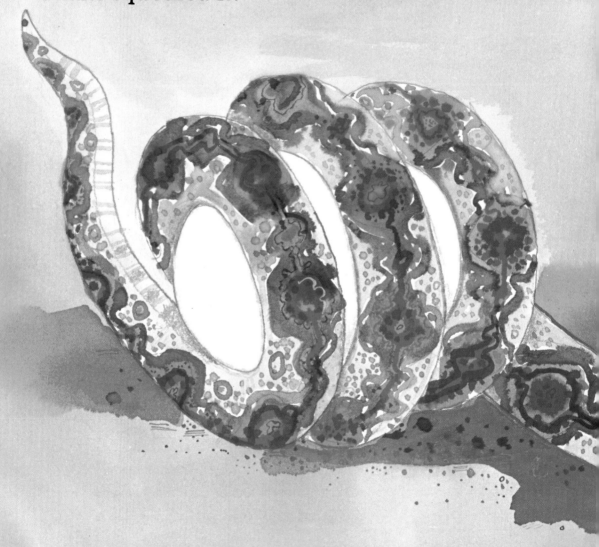

Zebra kicked it.

Flamingo flew high in the sky with it and
dropped it on the hard ground and still
it would not break.

Finally they all stood back to think.

While they were thinking the egg made
a croaking sound.
It wobbled and tiny cracks appeared.

Suddenly it burst open and out popped a grinning new crocodile, snapping his sharp white teeth.

The animals took one look and fled.
"I thought it was a bad egg,"
said stork as he went.

"Just wait till I've grown," said the little crocodile. Then he slipped into the water to join his brothers and sisters.

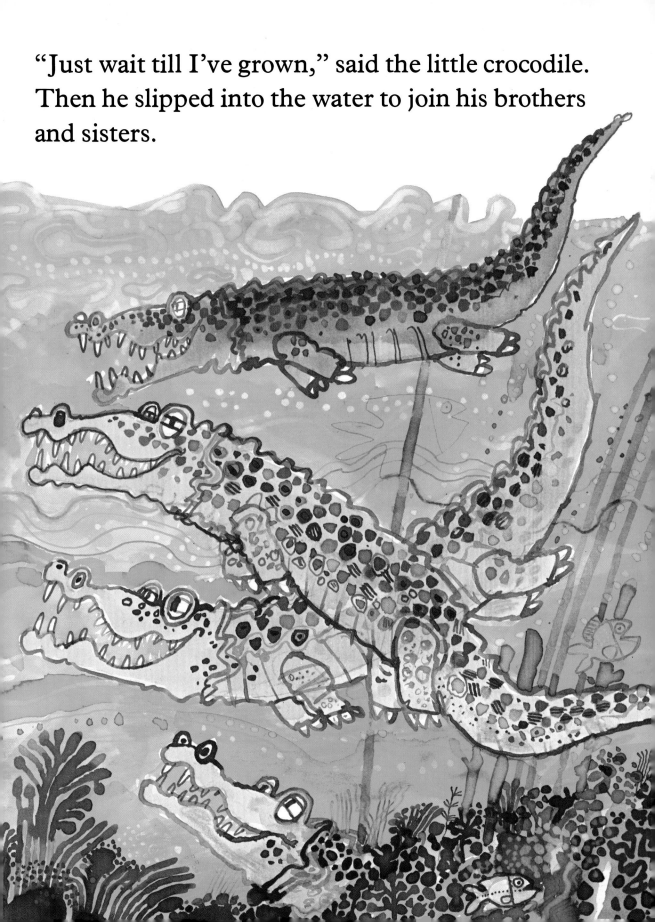

First published in 1986 by Macmillan Children's Books
a division of Macmillan Publishers Limited
20 New Wharf Road, London N1 9RR
Basingstoke and Oxford
Associated companies worldwide
www.panmacmillan.com

ISBN 0 333 41276 1

11 13 15 17 19 20 18 16 14 12

A CIP catalogue for this book is available
from the British Library.

Printed in China